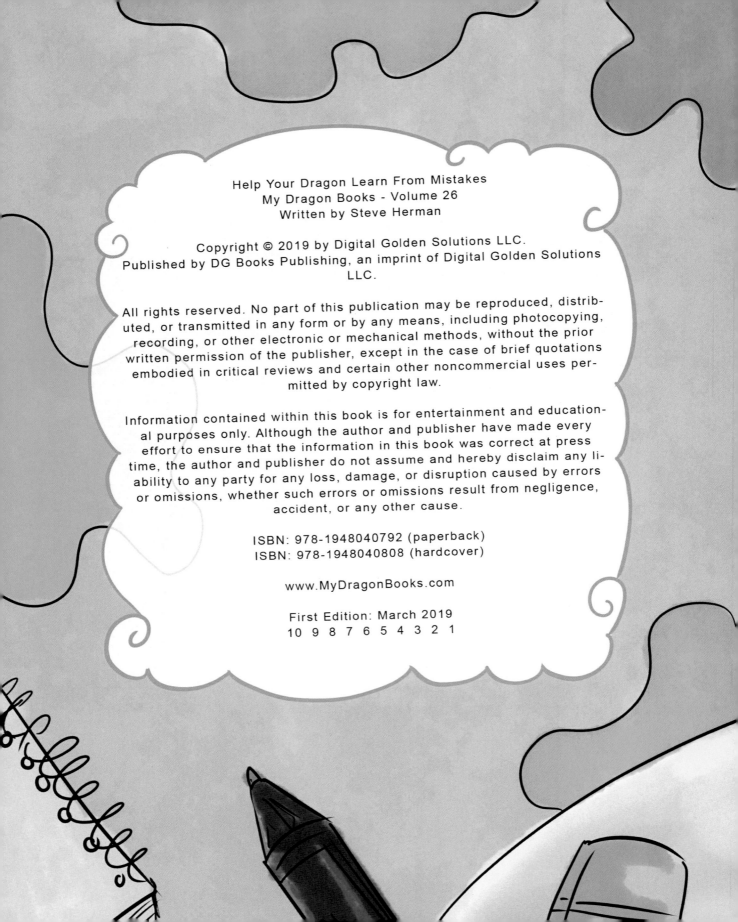

Help Your Dragon Learn From Mistakes
My Dragon Books - Volume 26
Written by Steve Herman

ISBN: 978-1948040792 (paperback)
ISBN: 978-1948040808 (hardcover)

www.MyDragonBooks.com

First Edition: March 2019
10 9 8 7 6 5 4 3 2 1

Help Your Dragon Learn From Mistakes

My Dragon Books - Volume 26

Steve Herman

A dragon is delightful
and a joy to have around,
But when I got my dragon,
one thing I quickly found...

One lesson Diggory learned was when he made the soccer team; He wanted to be perfect, but he was too extreme.

Once he missed the winning goal
and cost his team the game;
He hung his head in shame,
for he felt he was to blame.

He had made a small mistake,
so when he got his score,
Instead of a one hundred,
he had made a ninety-four.

Diggory Doo can breathe a flame,
but made a big mistake,
When he lit the candles
on a buddy's birthday cake.

He set the tablecloth on fire,
and though it happened long ago,
He talked about it all the time;
he couldn't let it go.

Diggory's teacher broke her arm;
he wished to make a card,
But dragons are quite clumsy,
and coloring is hard.

When he got outside the lines,
I heard my dragon say,
"Miss Smith will think my card is dumb,"
and he threw the card away.

Diggory Doo makes toy trains;
he uses model kits;
When a model didn't turn out right,
he smashed it all to bits.

"When it comes to making models," Diggory said, "I'm done; Unless they turn out perfect, it isn't any fun!"

One time Diggory ran a race, but when he didn't win,

He pouted and proclaimed that he would never race again.

"At least you know you're learning
what you didn't know before,
And that's what really matters
even more than what you score."

"Your teacher loves you, Diggory Doo!
You need not be afraid
That she wouldn't be enchanted
with a card that you had made,"

"Although you're no Van Gogh, your teacher is aware,
That you're a thoughtful dragon, when you show how much you care."

"I don't care, Diggory Doo,
how many times you blow it;
I'll still love you anyway,
and I want you to know it."

Since Diggory learned his lesson,
I know you can learn it, too;
You can learn from your mistakes,
like my dragon, Diggory Doo!

POTTY TRAIN
YOUR DRAGON
Steve Herman

TRAIN YOUR
ANGRY DRAGON
Steve Herman

THE MINDFUL
DRAGON
Steve Herman

THE YOGA
DRAGON
Steve Herman

DRAGON
& THE BULLY
Steve Herman

HAPPY BIRTHDAY
DRAGON
Steve Herman

TRAIN YOUR DRAGON
TO ACCEPT NO
Steve Herman

I GOT THIS!
Steve Herman

TRAIN YOUR DRAGON
TO BE KIND
Steve Herman

A DRAGON
With His Mouth ON FIRE
Steve Herman

TRAIN YOUR DRAGON
To Follow RULES
Steve Herman

TRAIN YOUR DRAGON
To Be RESPONSIBLE
Steve Herman

TRAIN YOUR DRAGON
To LOVE HIMSELF
Steve Herman

TRAIN YOUR DRAGON
To Understand CONSEQUENCES
Steve Herman

TEACH YOUR DRAGON
TO STOP LYING
Steve Herman

TEACH YOUR DRAGON
TO MAKE FRIENDS
Steve Herman

TEACH YOUR DRAGON
TO SHARE
Steve Herman

FIX YOUR DRAGON'S
ATTITUDE
Steve Herman

GET YOUR DRAGON
TO TRY NEW THINGS
Steve Herman

TEACH YOUR DRAGON
TO FOLLOW INSTRUCTIONS
Steve Herman

A DRAGON
CHRISTMAS
Steve Herman

HELP YOUR DRAGON
DEAL WITH ANXIETY
Steve Herman

TEACH YOUR DRAGON
MANNERS
Steve Herman

TEACH YOUR DRAGON
EMPATHY
Steve Herman

TEACH YOUR DRAGON
About DIVERSITY
Steve Herman

HELP YOUR DRAGON
Learn From **MISTAKES**
Steve Herman

HELP YOUR DRAGON
DEAL WITH **CHANGE**
Steve Herman

THE SAD **DRAGON**
A DRAGON BOOK ABOUT GRIEF AND LOSS
Steve Herman

DRAGON
SIBLING RIVALRY
Steve Herman

LIMIT YOUR DRAGON'S
SCREEN TIME
Steve Herman

DRAGON and HIS FRIEND
A Dragon Book About Autism
Steve Herman

TEACH YOUR DRAGON
GOOD **HYGIENE**
Steve Herman

TEACH YOUR DRAGON
ABOUT **STRANGER DANGER**
Steve Herman

HELP YOUR DRAGON
COPE WITH **TRAUMA**
Steve Herman

HELP YOUR DRAGON
OVERCOME **SEPARATION ANXIETY**
Steve Herman

TRAIN YOUR DRAGON
TO DO **HARD THINGS**
Steve Herman

TWO HOMES
FILLED WITH **LOVE**
Steve Herman

DRAGON'S MASK
Steve Herman

VIRTUAL LEARNING
DRAGON
Steve Herman

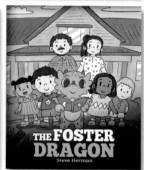

THE FOSTER
DRAGON
Steve Herman

A DRAGON
WITH **ADHD**
Steve Herman

GET YOUR DRAGON
TO EAT **HEALTHY FOOD**
Steve Herman

TEACH YOUR DRAGON
RESPECT
Steve Herman

TEACH YOUR DRAGON
BODY SAFETY
Steve Herman

THE BOSSY
DRAGON
Steve Herman

TEACH YOUR DRAGON
INTEGRITY
Steve Herman

BE A GOOD SPORT
DIGGORY DOO!
Steve Herman

A DRAGON
NEEDS HIS **SLEEP**
Steve Herman

A DRAGON
HAS TO **PERSEVERE**
Steve Herman

CELEBRATE
OUR **DIFFERENCES**
Steve Herman

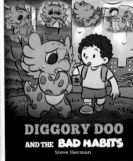

Made in the USA
Coppell, TX
10 October 2024

38472836R00026